Our heartfelt thanks to the many people who helped make *Lily + the Imaginary Zoo* a reality, especially the Clark, Decedue, Giardi, Levine and Silliman families, Karen MacPherson, Jean Silliman, Laura and Terry Smith, the Mayor's office and Mayor Thomas M. Menino.

Lily + the Imaginary Zoo
Published by:
Three Bean Press, LLC
P.O. Box 15386
Boston, MA 02215 U.S.A.
Orders@threebeanpress.com • http://threebeanpress.com

Publishers Cataloging-in-Publication Data
Clark, Seneca Teal
Giardi, Sandy
Lily + the Imaginary Zoo / by Seneca Clark and Sandy Giardi; illustrated by Julie Decedue.
p. cm.
Summary: Boston's animal statues come to life through the imagination of a little girl.
ISBN 0-9767276-1-7
[1. Children—Fiction. 2. Boston—Fiction. 3. Animals—Fiction.] I. Decedue, Julie, Ill. II. Title.
LCCN 2005902541

Printed in the U.S.A.

To my godson, Sebastien, with
his giant imagination - S.C.

For my daughter, Tessa - S.G.

To my nephews, Zach and Will,
my everyday inspiration - J.D.

Written by Seneca Clark and Sandy Giardi

Illustrated by Julie Decedue

On Saturday morning, LILY was ready to have some fun.

"MOMMY, can we go to
the ZOO today?"
Lily asked.

"What a great idea! We'll go right after we finish our errands," said Lily's mom.

BOSTon
POPZ!
cereal

Cit gO
GOPATS

“FIRST, we’ll return our library books.”

Lily and her mom entered the BOSTON PUBLIC LIBRARY and noticed a regal stone lion at the top of the stairs.

Lily's mom was distracted, searching for her library card, while Lily patted the STATUE'S head.

"Hello, LION! What are you doing here?" Lily asked.

bellowed the lion, springing to life. Lily was so surprised she jumped, and her books tumbled to the floor.

“Hello to you! I’m here because I love to READ,” said the lion.

“I love to read too,” said Lily.

“Then let’s read together.”

Lily and the lion plopped right down on the stairs and eagerly turned the pages of Lily’s favorite book.

At the end of the book, Lily said, “Thanks for the story, Lion. My mom is waiting—we have to go buy a birthday present now.”

“Bye-bye, Lily.”
“Bye-bye, Lion.”

purred the lion, as he turned to stone once again.

Next, Lily and her mother walked through COPLEY SQUARE. Lily spotted a metal tortoise and a hare.

While her mother gazed up at TRINITY CHURCH,
Lily tapped the tortoise on his shell. The tortoise slowly turned his head and smiled.

"Hello, TORTOISE! What are you doing here?"
"I'm trying to win the race," he droned steadily.
Suddenly, the HARE interrupted, "Catch me if you can!"

As they ran, their feet struck the pavement,

"C'mon, Tortoise.
Hurry up!" giggled Lily.

Lily cheered as she crossed the finish line before the tortoise and the hare. By then she was HUNGRY.

"So long, Tortoise. See you later, Hare. Thanks for the race!" she called over her shoulder. "My mom says it's time for our picnic lunch."

"Bye-bye, Lily," they chorused.

and they returned to where they started.

While Lily's mom unfolded a blanket in the PUBLIC GARDEN, Lily visited the sculpture of Mrs. Mallard and her ducklings. Lily stroked the mother duck's shiny, well-loved head.

"Hello, DUCK!" said Lily.

Mrs. Mallard answered.

"What are you doing here?"
Lily asked.

"We're getting ready for a swim. Meet my babies," honked Mrs. Mallard, "Jack, Kack, Lack, Mack, Nack, Ouack, Pack and Quack."

"Will you please join us for lunch first?" invited Lily.

Quack Quack
NORTH END
Pastry Shop
North End Pastry
Charles
River Co.
H2O

Quack Quack

Waddling to the blanket, the ducks pecked their sandwiches into pieces and shared Lily's cookies. After lunch, Lily explained, "My mom says we're off to the dry cleaners. Thanks for visiting!"

"Bye-bye, Lily."
"Bye-bye, Ducks."

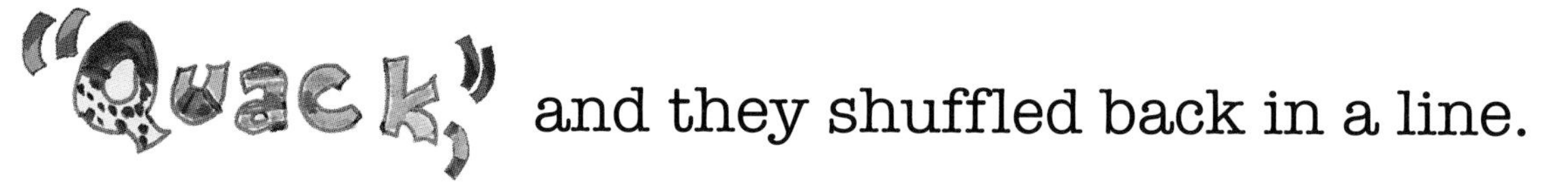

and they shuffled back in a line.

Crossing BOSTON COMMON, Lily spotted children splashing in the FROG POND fountain.

"MOM, can I put my feet in?"

Lily pleaded.

"Of course you can," said her mother as she saw a friend and waved hello.

Freedom Trail
RED SOX

Lily was happy to see a frog statue squatting at the edge of the fountain and she reached down to splash him. “Hello, FROG!”

he CROAKED, smiling.

“Watch where you’re splashing!”

Lily squealed with delight as the frog leaped toward her. “What are you doing here?” Lily asked.

“We’re having playtime. Fancy a dance, little girl?” he asked, holding out his webbed hand. The music began, and all of the other frogs joined in.

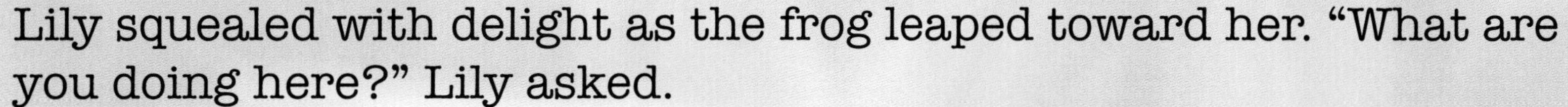

"My mom is calling. I have to run. But I had fun!" said Lily.

"Me too," said the frog.
"Thanks for the dance!"

"Bye, Lily."
"Bye, Frogs."

and the frogs bounded back to their posts.

Lily skipped all the way to the cleaners and spied yet another animal statue in front of OLD CITY HALL. It was a DONKEY!

While Lily's mom looked for her dry cleaning ticket, Lily approached the donkey and nuzzled his muzzle.

the donkey BRAYED, baring a TOOTHY SMILE.

"Hello, Donkey! What are you doing here?"

"I'm guarding the courtyard. Care to go for a ride? Climb on!"

“WHEE! Faster, faster!” she called as the donkey trotted around the square. After a few laps, Lily looked to her mother. Sadly, it was time to go.

“Thanks for the ride!”
“Any time, Lily!”
“Bye, Donkey.” “Bye-bye, Lily.”

he said, and returned to his stubborn pose.

Back in the car, now loaded with new library books, birthday presents and freshly cleaned clothes, Lily's mom said, "We've finished our errands. The next stop is the ZOO!"

Lily let out a big yawn.

"That's okay! I've made enough animal friends for one day."

A few words about the public art featured....

St. Gaudens' Lions, Dartmouth Street entrance, McKim Building, Boston Public Library. Artist Louis St. Gaudens created the beautiful twin lions that hold court on either side of the entrance's marble staircase. The lions, placed in position in 1891, are crafted in unpolished Siena marble and are a memorial to the 2nd and 20th Massachusetts Regiments of the Civil War. Louis St. Gaudens was the brother of Augustus St. Gaudens who sculpted Beacon Hill's Shaw Memorial.

Tortoise and Hare, Copley Square. Installed May 19, 1995. Nancy Schön's bronze on brick statue is aptly placed near the finish of the Boston Marathon. The Newton native and lifelong athlete created this sculpture as a testament to marathon runners, as well as for children who can learn much from the fable about achieving success at a slow and steady pace. The sculpture was sponsored by the Friends of Copley Square and completed to commemorate the 100th running of the Boston Marathon.

Make Way for Ducklings, Boston Public Garden, closest to the corner of Beacon and Charles streets. Installed Oct. 4, 1987. Another work by sculptor Nancy Schön, this very popular bronze on Old Boston cobblestones is based on the drawings of author Robert McCloskey who, through his story about Mr. and Mrs. Mallard and their eight ducklings, allowed children everywhere to spend some time in the Public Garden. To learn more about the prolific public art of Nancy Schön, visit www.schon.com.

Frog statues, Frog Pond and Tadpole Playground, Boston Common, closest to Beacon and Park streets. In 1996, the beloved Frog Pond (which was officially established in 1848 for the Great Water Celebration) underwent an overall renovation by the Copley Wolff Design Group. Sculptor David Phillips' bronze frog statues, which decorate the Pond and the nearby whimsical Tadpole Playground, are a tremendous draw for children of all ages in all seasons, whether it's for skating in the winter or splashing in the summer. Phillips' studio is based in Medford, Mass.; his work can be viewed at www.phillipssculpture.com.

Donkey sculpture, in front of Old City Hall, 45 School St. The lovable bronze donkey, which was created by an unidentified artist at an art studio in Florence, Italy, was installed in 2000. Representing the Democratic party, the donkey symbolizes the political history of Old City Hall, as the majority of all mayors who served there were Democrats.

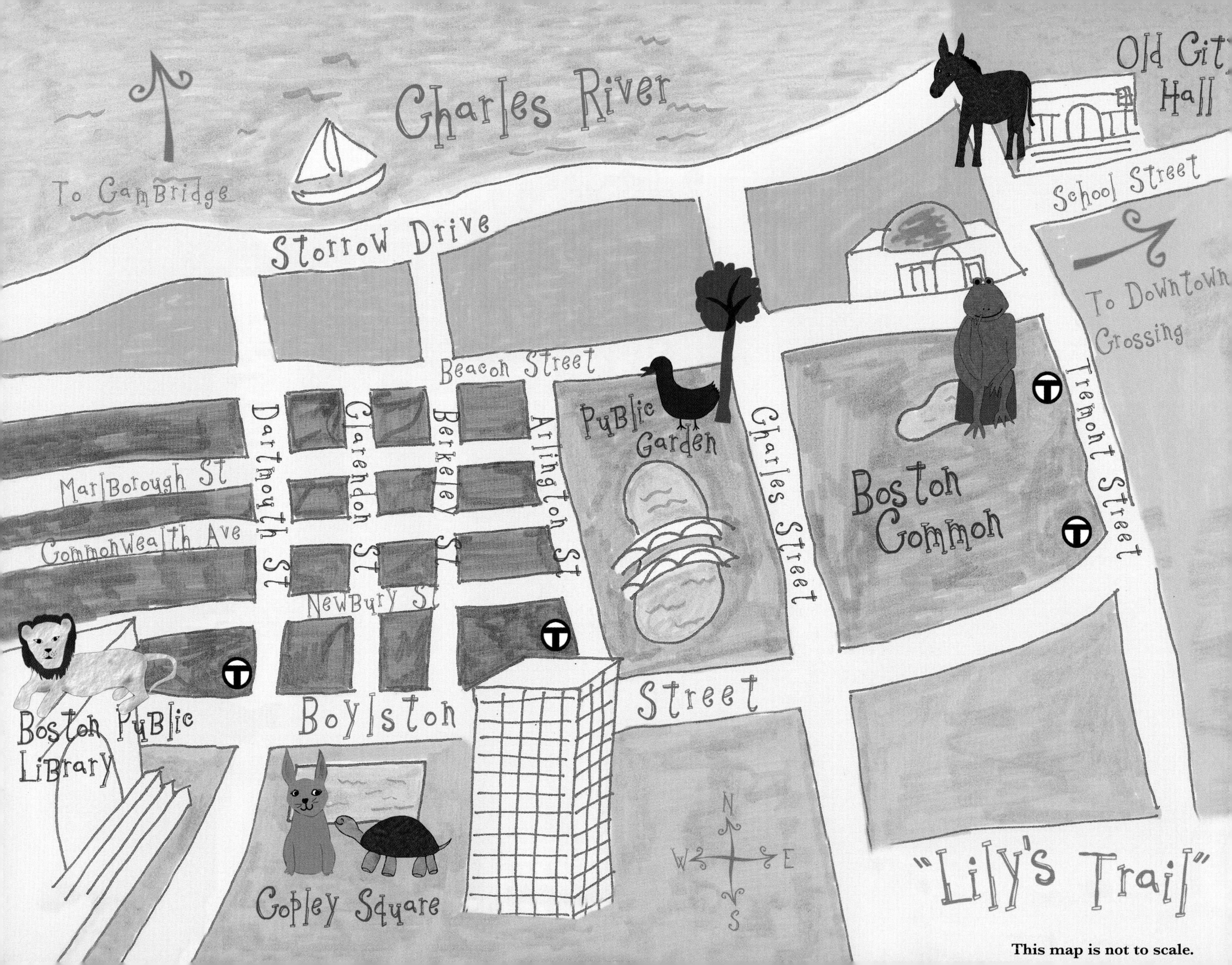

This map is not to scale.